FROM DINOSAUR TO DINOSTAR
TYRANNOSAURUS REX

CAPTAIN T-REX

Devoted and fearless leader of the Dinostars. Dedicated to exploring Space and keeping his team safe.

- Favourite colour: **Red**
- Least favourite food: **Beans**
- Fastest speed travelled:
  2×10^8 metres per second
- Did you know?
  He is the oldest Dinostar by 5 months

B.U.G.

| ROLO | TOPS | CAPTAIN T-REX | DIPPY | STEG |
| SCIENTIST | FIRST COMMANDER | | NAVIGATOR | MECHANIC |

For Ned Mantle

First published 2016 by Macmillan Children's Books
an imprint of Pan Macmillan,
20 New Wharf Road, London N1 9RR
Associated companies throughout the world

www.panmacmillan.com

ISBN: 978–1–5098–2915–6

Text & Illustrations copyright © Ben Mantle 2016

3 5 7 9 8 6 4 2

A CIP catalogue record for this book is available from the British Library.

Printed in China

DINOSTARS
AND THE
PLANET PLUNDERING PIRATES

by Ben Mantle

MACMILLAN CHILDREN'S BOOKS

In the deepest, darkest reaches of the Dinostar galaxy,
the Dinopod shut down its boosters and eased to a stop.

"Are we there yet?" asked Tops.

Dippy looked confused.
"We should be looking right at Planet Bellu . . .
But it's gone!"

"How can a planet totally disappear?"asked Rolo.
"And why?" said Captain T-Rex. "Four have gone
missing this week. Something very strange is happening."

At that moment Steg entered the control room carrying his latest invention. "Say hello to the GUZZLE-ATOR!" he beamed.

"It makes any meal bigger! Just point it at the food and set the dial to how hungry you are."

"Let's see!" said Dippy, holding up the doughnuts.
Steg set the growth ray to MEGA HUNGRY.

ZZZAAAAPP!

"Sorry Dippy!" shouted Steg.
"My aim isn't very good."

Dippy's neck
began to shake,

and it grew longer . . .

and longer . . .

and LONGER!

The computer screen started to flash with a warning.
"Look!" said Tops. "Another planet is moving."

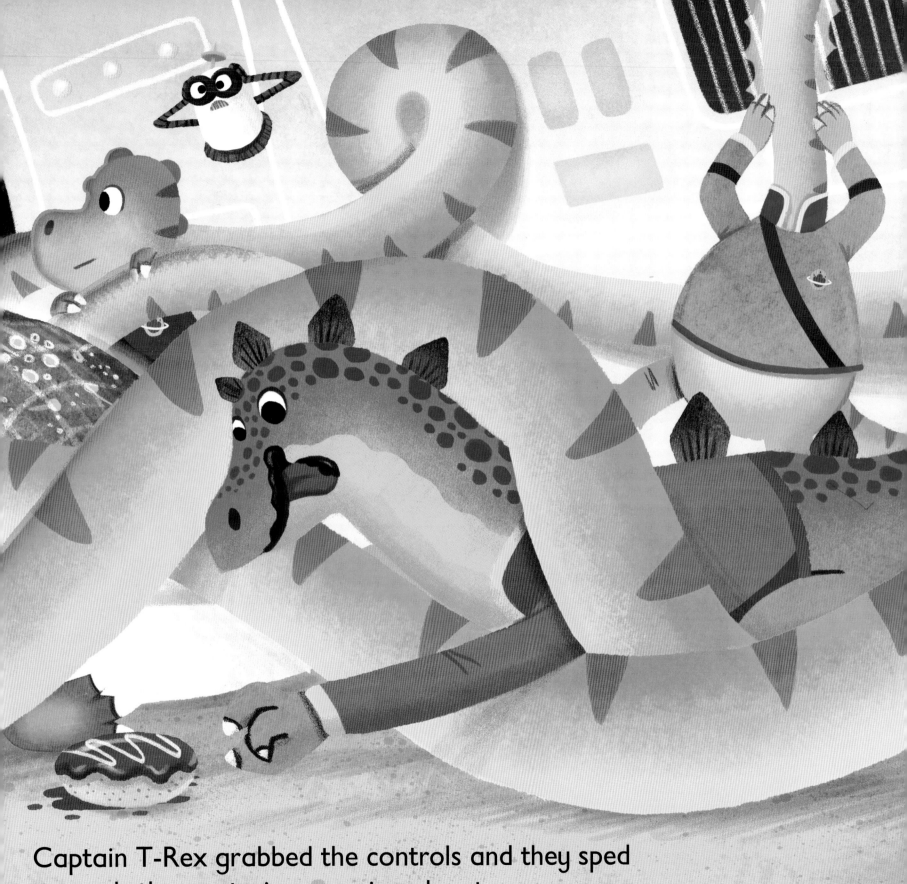

Captain T-Rex grabbed the controls and they sped towards the mysterious moving planet.

"It's **SPACE PIRATES!**" cried Tops.
"And they're stealing the planet!"

Dippy's nose began to tingle.
"I think I'm going to
AH . . . AH . . . AH . . .

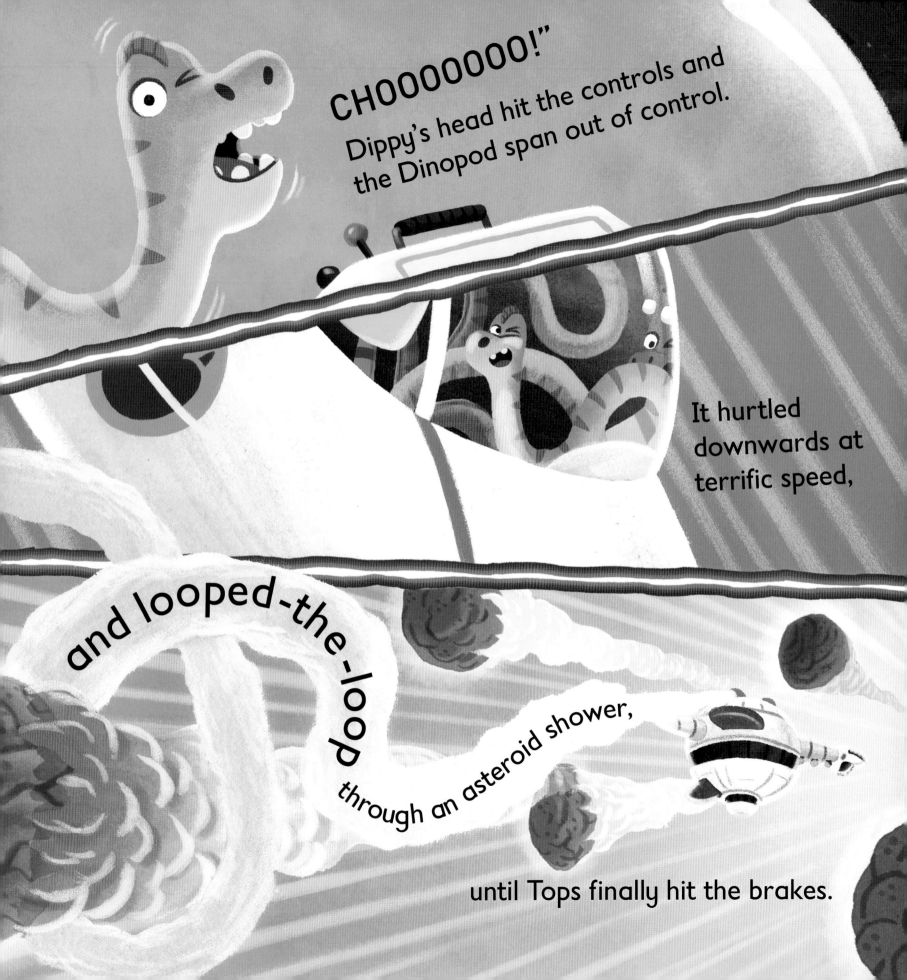

CHOOOOOOO!"
Dippy's head hit the controls and the Dinopod span out of control.

It hurtled downwards at terrific speed,

and looped-the-loop

through an asteroid shower,

until Tops finally hit the brakes.

The pirates and the planet had vanished.
"My head!" moaned Dippy.

"Thank goodness!" said Steg. "Dippy's neck is almost back to normal. The effect of the GUZZLE-ATOR must only last for a short time."

"Captain!" shouted Tops. "I've found this information on the pirates."

WANTED!

Led by Captain Clops, the Dreadnaughts are a fearsome and greedy bunch of perilous plunderers. They will stop at nothing to steal every big shiny treasure in the universe.

Suddenly everything turned darker.

"The Dreadnaughts are stealing the sun!" shouted Dippy.

"They must have found a wormhole into our galaxy," said Rolo.

"And they're taking the planets back to *their* galaxy."

"A what hole?" asked Steg.

Rolo pointed to her screen. "A wormhole is like a shortcut between two far-away parts of Space," she said. "But it could close at any time and you would be stuck on the wrong side forever!"

Captain T-Rex sprang into action. "We need to get our sun back before it's too late," he said. "Dinostars, follow that pirate ship!"

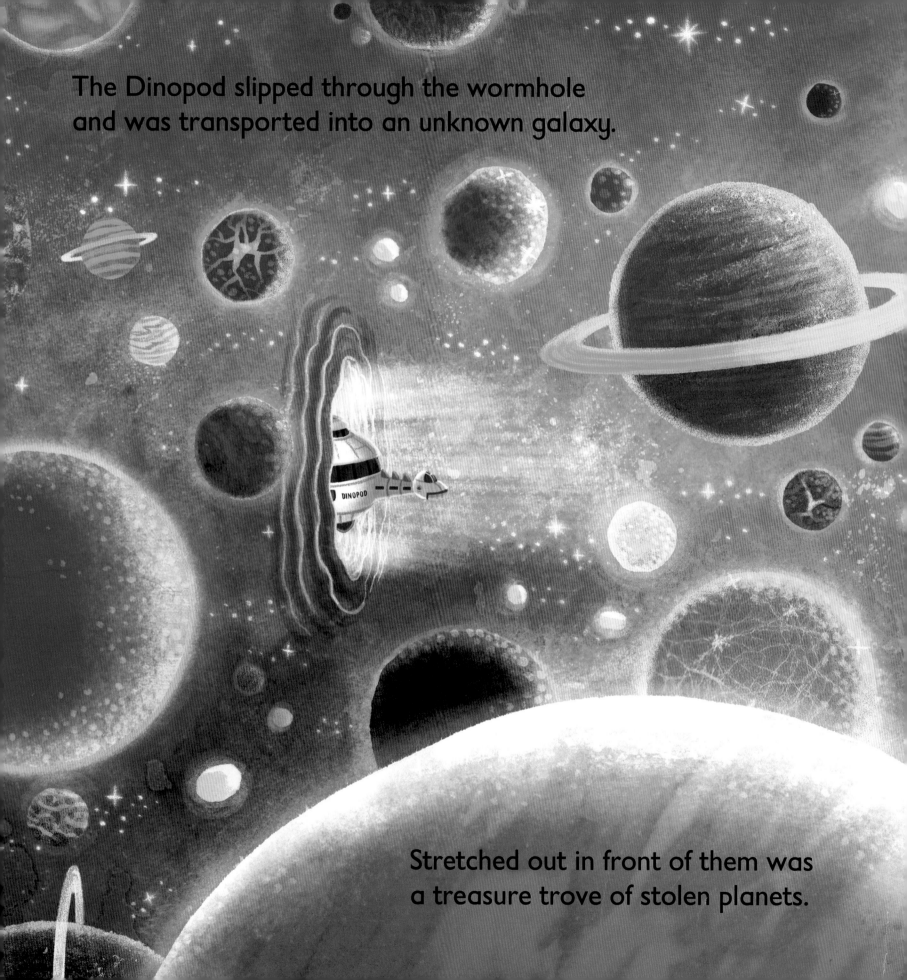

The Dinopod slipped through the wormhole and was transported into an unknown galaxy.

Stretched out in front of them was a treasure trove of stolen planets.

"Wow!" whispered Rolo.
"So this is where all the planets
have gone," said Captain T-Rex.

"Doughnut anybody?" offered Steg.

"That's it! I have a plan," said Captain T-Rex. "Steg, hand me
the GUZZLE-ATOR. And I'm going to need that doughnut."

Captain T-Rex jumped into his Pteroplane.
"I'm going to distract the pirates while the rest of
you get our planets back," he instructed his team.

The captain switched on the boosters.
"Dinostars, Space needs our help!"

"Goodbye candy sprinkled ring
doughnut," whispered Steg.

Captain T-Rex flew straight towards the pirate ship. "Intruder!" shouted Captain Clops. "After him."

With the pirates distracted, the Dinostars started dragging their planets through the wormhole.

The Dreadnaughts closed
in on the Pteroplane . . .

just as the Dinostars
pulled their sun back
to where it belonged.

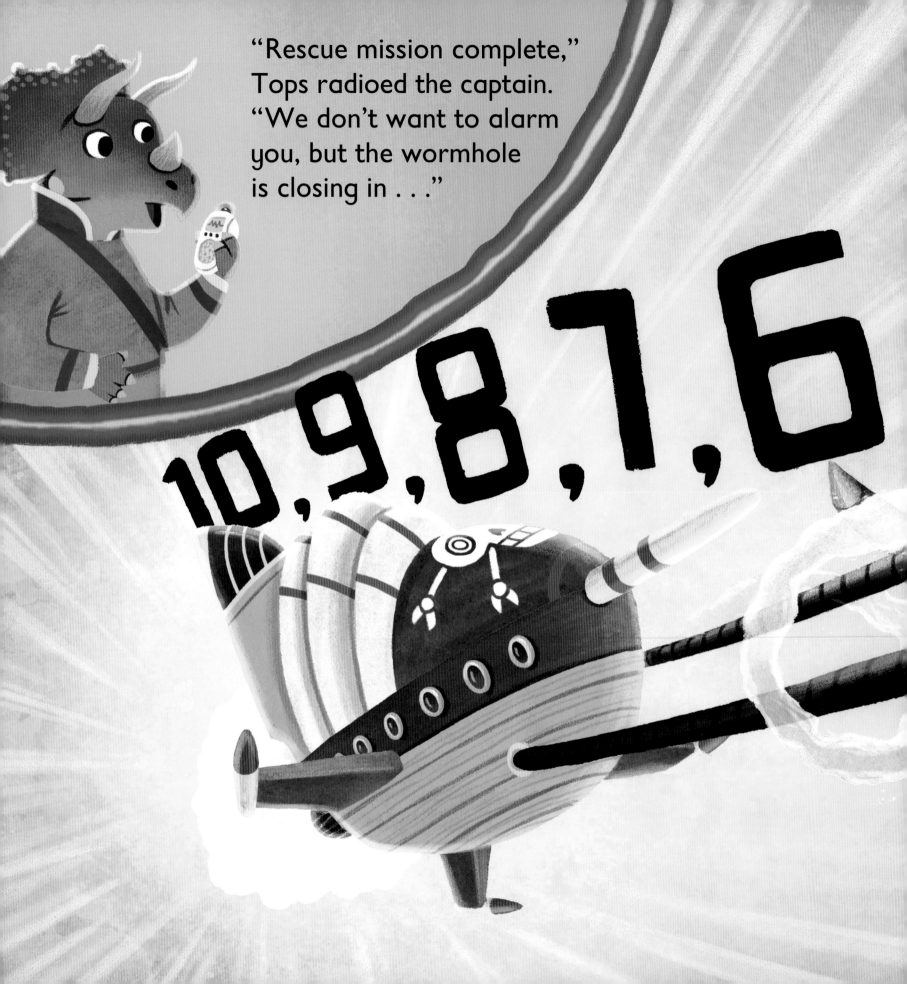

"Rescue mission complete," Tops radioed the captain. "We don't want to alarm you, but the wormhole is closing in . . ."

10, 9, 8, 7, 6

Captain T-Rex set the GUZZLE-ATOR to RAVENOUS and fired the doughnut at the wormhole.

3,

The doughnut grew bigger and bigger,

2,

and wedged open the shrinking wormhole,

1,

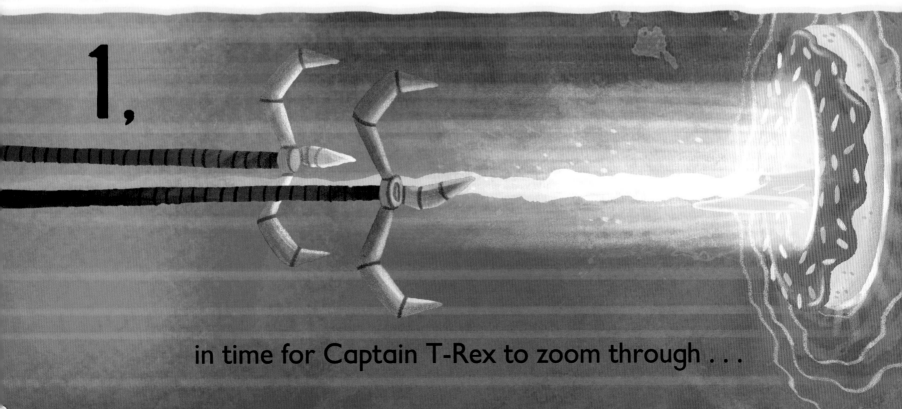

in time for Captain T-Rex to zoom through . . .

before it closed on the pirate ship behind him.

"Curse you Dinostars!"
Captain Clops snarled.
"We'll be back."

"Good work, team," said Captain T-Rex
when he was safely back on board the Dinopod.
The Dinostars gazed at all their planets back in place.

Steg picked up the GUZZLE-ATOR.
"I don't know about you," he smiled . . .

"but I'm RAVENOUS!"

ROLO'S SPACE FACTS

WORMHOLES

- Wormholes are openings that connect two completely different parts of Space and time.

- Scientists believe you could go through a wormhole and come out the other side anywhere in the universe – even millions of light years away!

- Some scientists even think that wormholes could allow us to travel through time.

- But beware! Wormholes are unstable and could suddenly collapse, trapping you on the wrong side forever.

- Humans have not discovered a real wormhole yet, so until they do it's just an idea that they're trying to prove.